READ WITH
Biff,
Chip &
Kipper

The Strange Box

Written by Roderick Hunt
and illustrated by Alex Brychta

OXFORD
UNIVERSITY PRESS

Before reading

- Read the back cover text and page 4. How do you think things might change when the children find the strange box?
- Look at page 5. The box is part of an ancient machine. What powers might it once have had?

After reading

- What unusual things happened whenever the sinister man appeared?
- Why do you think Mr Mortlock called him 'the enemy'?

Book quiz

1 Who runs the second-hand stall at the school fair?
  a Wilma's mum
  b Mrs May
  c Floppy
2 How much money does the sinister man offer Nadim for the box?
3 How does Mr Mortlock get rid of the sinister man in the end?

See p45 for the book quiz answers!

Introduction

A long time has passed since the children have been on a magic key adventure. In fact, they have almost forgotten the last time the key glowed.

Biff and Chip are now ten, Kipper is eight, and Wilma has started secondary school.

When Chip discovers a strange old box in his room, things begin to change forever.

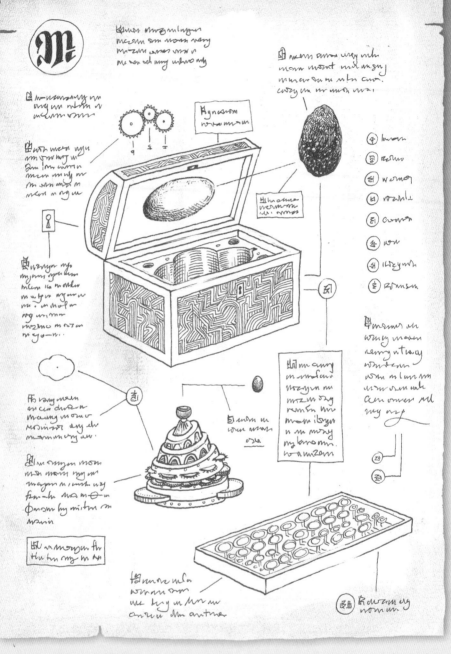

The Parts of the TimeWeb

"The TimeWeb is an ancient machine. It acts like an eye looking into the past ... See, it has four parts; the Hub ... the Matrix ... the Cell ... and the box is the case which connects it all together."

Theodore Mortlock – Time Guardian

Chapter 1

Chip found the old box on top of his wardrobe. It had been there for years. He'd just forgotten about it.

He took the box down, blew the dust off, and looked at it curiously.

"Come and see this, Biff," he called.

The box was made of heavy metal and had strange markings on it.

"We found the magic key inside it," said Chip. "Do you remember?" He scratched the lid with his finger-nail.

"It's rusty," Biff said. "But the rust is an odd, green colour."

They took the box downstairs and Biff rubbed it with a scouring pad. Under the green rust, the metal shone with different colours.

"It looks like oil when it's spilled on water," said Biff.

Kipper came into the kitchen. He flung his football kit on the floor, went to the fridge and poured himself a glass of orange juice.

"Hey! What a weird-looking box," he said.

"It had the magic key in it," replied Chip, "but it's not much use. The inside is all peculiar. Look!"

The box was empty, but inside were metal grooves and slots. It looked as if something complicated had once fitted exactly into it.

"We've no idea what it is, or what it was used for," said Biff.

Chip left the box on the worktop and they all went upstairs.

What they didn't see was the faint glow that seeped out through the half-shut lid of the box.

Chapter 2

The big event of the weekend was the
school fair. The money raised at the fair
was going to buy IT equipment.

Mum had been busy making cakes to sell.
Biff, Chip and Kipper had filled a bag with
old toys and games for the toy stall.

That Saturday, Wilma's mum came to the house to collect things for her second-hand stall. Wilma was helping her to run it.

"We've not much for you," said Mum. "There's a vase, some china cats and a picture that none of us likes."

Chip spotted the old box on the worktop. "How about this? Somebody might want to buy it," he said. He looked at Biff and Kipper. "We don't want it, do we?"

Biff and Kipper shook their heads.

And so Wilma's mum took the box to sell on her stall.

After that, the trouble began.

Chapter 3

L ater the family went to the supermarket. When they got home, Floppy was barking loudly. A window had been broken and the kitchen door was open.

"Someone's broken in," gasped Dad.

"Oh no!" exclaimed Mum. "What have they taken?"

They looked round to see what had been stolen, but nothing was missing.

The only strange thing was that the house felt very cold, and the glass from a broken light bulb lay on the floor.

"Maybe Floppy saw them off," said Biff.

"It's very odd," thought Chip. "I wonder what they were after?"

Later, Biff called Chip to her room.

"I know this sounds silly," she began, "but do you think it was a good idea to give the old box away? We did find the key in it."

"Why not? The key's still safe, isn't it?"

Biff opened a drawer where the key was hidden in a pair of her old socks.

"Of course it is," she said.

Chapter 4

Wilma found it strange to be back in her old school. Last year she had moved up to the secondary school.

Now she was back helping her mum to run a stall at the school fair.

She enjoyed setting up the stall. She put large objects at the back, and smaller ones at the front.

She had a surprise when she picked up the old box.

"It's really heavy," she said.

In the end, she put the box next to a brass dish and the china cats.

Wilma's mum was on a separate table. She was selling the more valuable items.

Everyone was pleased to see Mrs May at the fair. She had retired two years ago and had come back to open it.

"I want you all to spend lots of money," joked Mrs May, "and make this the best school fair ever. I now declare the fair open."

People rushed to the stalls to try and get a bargain. On Wilma's stall many of the items sold quickly, but nobody seemed interested in the old box.

Then something strange happened. It felt as if an icy wind had blown through the hall. Then there was a loud pop. One of the strip lights had exploded. Then the lights flickered and went dim.

"A power cut," someone groaned.

Mr Mortlock, the caretaker, hurried into the hall, but then the lights came back on again.

"How odd!" said Wilma's mum.

Chapter 5

Nadim came to the stall with Wilf and
Neena. He picked up the old box and
opened it.

"I like this, Wilma. How much?" he asked.

"Five pounds?" replied Wilma hopefully.

"Fine," said Nadim, handing Wilma the
money.

"But I'd like to buy that box, too," said a
voice behind them.

Nadim spun round. The voice was icy and sinister. It belonged to a tall man in a long coat. He had pale, waxy skin, bright green eyes and very black hair.

The man's eyes were so cold and piercing that Wilma shuddered.

"I'm sorry, the box is sold," she said, even though the man scared her.

The man stared at Nadim. "I'll give you thirty pounds. That's six times what you paid for it," he said.

Nadim imagined that if a snake could talk, its voice would sound just like this man's. But something made Nadim want to keep the box, whatever the man offered him, so he shook his head.

"You stupid boy," the man hissed. "You have no use for the box. But I have. All right, I'll give you fifty pounds."

Biff and Chip gasped. Fifty pounds was a lot for a useless old box.

"Take the money," urged Chip.

Out of the corner of his eye, Nadim saw Mr Mortlock shaking his head.

Nadim's heart beat fast. It was hard to breathe. He thought what he could do with fifty pounds, but something told him not to sell the box to this man.

"Sorry," he said. "It's not for sale."

The man opened his mouth to speak, but Mr Mortlock moved close to Nadim.

"Is everything all right?" Mr Mortlock asked in a firm voice.

The man stared at Nadim with lizard-like eyes. They made the hair rise on the back of Nadim's neck.

"Er...yes," said Nadim. "I think so."

The man turned sharply and strode away. Mr Mortlock spoke quietly to himself.

"So, the enemy has come!" he said.

Chapter 6

Every Saturday afternoon Biff, Chip and Kipper took Floppy for a walk. They ran home quickly and put Floppy on his lead. Then they walked back to school to meet their friends.

They wanted to talk about the scary man. Who was he? Why did he want the box so badly, and what did Mr Mortlock have to do with it?

They met up with Wilf, Wilma, Nadim and Neena outside the school.

As they walked home together, Chip noticed that Nadim was holding the old box tightly under his arm.

They all talked about the sinister man who had come to the stall. The thought of him made them shudder.

"Ugh! That weird man who wanted to buy that box ..." Wilma began.

Chip cut in. "But you turned down fifty pounds, Nadim," he said. "I would have taken the money just to get rid of him."

Nadim shrugged. "There was something about him. I couldn't let him have it."

Suddenly Floppy stopped and growled.

"Has it turned chilly?" asked Kipper.

Then, as they turned into the park, there he was – the strange man. He was standing in front of them, blocking their way.

"I want that box," he hissed. "It is not yours, it's mine. Give it to me."

Chip's heart gave a leap. "It was you who broke into our house," he shouted. "You were looking for the box."

But the man just stared at Nadim.

Nadim felt he couldn't turn away from
the cold gaze of the man's green eyes. He
held the box out, and the man's gloved hand
reached out to take it.

"No!" shouted Biff. She snatched the box
away just as the gloved fingers closed on it.
The man lunged at her, but she threw the
box back to Nadim.

"Run!" shouted Biff.

They ran in a group, Nadim in the middle with the box under his arm. As if from nowhere, the man was in front of them.

"That's impossible," gasped Wilf.

The man stretched out his arms as if he was pulling them towards him.

Behind them came the sound of running footsteps. It was Mr Mortlock.

He stood in front of the man and pointed something at him.

There was a bright flash and a loud, crackling sound.

The man dissolved into a green flame that curled and twisted into a serpent-like shape.

Then, like a firework, the shape turned into sparks and tiny shards of flame. They shot into the air, with a hiss and a whoosh.

"The time has come sooner than I wanted," shouted Mr Mortlock. "The enemy is here, but we still have the box. Run, all of you. Run through the door."

It was as if a shimmering heat haze had risen in front of the trees. In the centre of it was a blue door.

"It's a door in the landscape," gasped Chip. "It's like the one in the magic key adventures."

The door swung open. There was only one thing to do ...

... they ran through it.

Now what?

What will the children find on the other side of the door? Are they in danger?

Who was the strange man and why did he want the box so badly?

How could the man simply disappear in a shower of sparks? Was he a human?

And who is Mr Mortlock? Why did he say, "So the enemy has come"? What did he mean?

Find out in the next book:

Beyond the Door

There isn't a moment to lose!

Chip

School: Ortree Primary

Age: 10   *Year:* 6

Likes: art

Dislikes: quarrelling

Special ability: sense of humour

Kipper

School: Ortree Primary

Age: 8   *Year:* 4

Likes: reading

Dislikes: finishing things

Special ability: telling jokes

Biff

School: Ortree Primary

Age: 10   *Year:* 6

Likes: making things

Dislikes: wearing skirts

Special ability: reliable and brave

Wilf

School: Ortree Primary

Age: 10   *Year:* 6

Likes: skateboarding

Dislikes: being bossed around

Special ability: acting and
                    performing

Neena

School: Ortree Primary
Age: 11   *Year*: 6
Likes: making music
Dislikes: swimming
Special ability: being helpful

Nadim

School: Ortree Primary
Age: 11   *Year*: 6
Likes: gadgets and computers
Dislikes: singing
Special ability: solving problems

Wilma

School: Walton High School
Age: 12   *Year*: 7
Likes: nice clothes
Dislikes: mess
Special ability: common sense

Floppy

School: Obedience Training
Age: 12   *Dog years*: 84
Likes: sleeping
Dislikes: baths
Special ability: loyal and
                   protective

Glossary

exclaimed *(page 14)* Shouted or cried out in excitement or surprise. *"Oh no!" exclaimed Mum. "What have they taken?"*

lunged *(page 32)* Moved forward quickly and suddenly. *The man lunged at her ...*

piercing *(page 23)* A piercing stare makes you feel as if the person can see right into your mind. It is a very uncomfortable feeling. *The man's eyes were so cold and piercing that Wilma shuddered.*

seeped *(page 10)* Oozed out slowly (usually used about light or water). *What they didn't see was the faint glow that seeped out through the half-shut lid of the box.*

serpent *(page 34)* Another word for a snake. *The man dissolved into a green flame that curled and twisted into a serpent-like shape.*

sinister *(page 29)* Something that is scary or threatening. *They all talked about the sinister man who had come to the stall.*

valuable *(page 18)* Something of great value – usually either worth a lot of money or of great personal importance. *Wilma's mum ... was selling the more valuable items.*

Thesaurus: Another word for ...

sinister *(page 29)* menacing, intimidating, threatening, ominous.

Have you read them all yet?

Level 11:

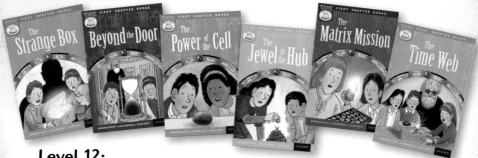

Level 12:

Time Runners

Tyler: His Story

A Jack and Three Queens

Mission Victory

The Enigma Plot

The Thief Who Stole Nothing

More great fiction from Oxford University Press:

www.winnie-the-witch.com

www.dinosaurcove.co.uk

About the Authors

Roderick Hunt MBE – creator of best-loved characters Biff, Chip, Kipper, Floppy and their friends. His first published stories were those he told his two sons at bedtime. Rod lives in Oxfordshire, in a house not unlike the house in the Magic Key adventures. In 2008, Roderick received an MBE for services to education, particularly literacy.

Roderick Hunt's son **David Hunt** was brought up on his father's stories and knows the world of Biff, Chip and Kipper intimately. His love of history and a good story has sparked many new ideas, resulting in the *Time Chronicles* series. David has had a successful career in the theatre, most recently working on scripts for Jude Law's *Hamlet* and *Henry V*, as well as Derek Jacobi's *Twelfth Night*.

Joint creator of the best-loved characters Biff, Chip, Kipper, Floppy and their friends, **Alex Brychta MBE** has brought each one to life with his fabulous illustrations, which are known and loved in many schools today. Following the Russian occupation of Czechoslovakia, Alex Brychta moved with his family from Prague to London. He studied graphic design and animation, before moving to the USA where he worked on animation for Sesame Street. Since then he has devoted many years of his career to *Oxford Reading Tree*, bringing detail, magic and humour to every story! In 2012 Alex received an MBE for services to children's literature.

Roderick Hunt and Alex Brychta won the prestigious Outstanding Achievement Award at the Education Resources Awards in 2009.

Levelling info for parents

What do the levels mean?

Read with Biff Chip & Kipper First Chapter Books have been designed by educational experts to help children develop as readers.

Each book is carefully levelled to allow children to make gradual progress and to feel confident and enjoy reading.

The Oxford Levels you will see on these books are used by teachers and are based on years of research in schools. Below is a summary of what each Oxford Level means, so that you can help your child to improve and enjoy their reading.

The books at Level 11 (Brown Book Band):

At this level, the sentence structures are becoming longer and more complex. The story plot may be more involved and there is a wider vocabulary. However, the proportion of unknown words used per paragraph/page is still carefully controlled to help build their reading stamina and allow children to read independently.

This level mostly covers characterisation through characters' actions and words rather than through description. The story may be organised in various ways, e.g. chronologically, thematically, sequentially, as relevant to the text type and subject.

The books at Level 12 (Grey Book Band):

At this level, the sentences are becoming more varied in structure and length. Though still straightforward, more inference may be required, e.g. in dialogue to work out who is speaking. Again, the story may be organised in various ways: chronologically, thematically, sequentially, etc., so that children can reflect on how the organisation helps the reader to understand the text.

The *Times Chronicles* books are also ideal for older children who feel less confident and need more practice in order to build stamina. The text is written to be age and ability appropriate, but also engaging, motivating and funny, making them a pleasure for children to read at this stage of their reading development.

OXFORD
UNIVERSITY PRESS

Great Clarendon Street, Oxford, OX2 6DP,
United Kingdom

Oxford University Press is a department of the University of Oxford.
It furthers the University's objective of excellence in research, scholarship,
and education by publishing worldwide. Oxford is a registered trade mark
of Oxford University Press in the UK and in certain other countries

Text © Roderick Hunt and David Hunt

Text written by David Hunt, based on the original characters
created by Roderick Hunt and Alex Brychta

Illustrations © Alex Brychta

The moral rights of the authors have been asserted

Database rights Oxford University Press (maker)

First published 2010
This edition published in 2014

British Library Cataloguing in Publication Data
Data available

978-0-19-273905-6

1 3 5 7 9 10 8 6 4 2

Paper used in the production of this book is a natural, recyclable product
made from wood grown in sustainable forests. The manufacturing process
conforms to the environmental regulations of the country of origin.

Printed in China

Acknowledgements
The publisher and authors would like to thank the following for their
permission to reproduce photographs and other copyright material:
end papers: Omela/Shutterstock; P38tl: Iguasu/Shutterstock; P38tr:
Eric Gevaert/Shutterstock; P38ml: Mikhail/Shutterstock; P38br:
Leigh Prather/Shutterstock

Book quiz answers

1 a

2 At first he offers Nadim £30, then £50 when he turns that down.

3 He points something at the sinister man, which makes him dissolve into a green flame.